To the magic of belief

All inquiries should be addressed to:

Mitten Press
An imprint of Ann Arbor Media Group LLC
2500 S. State Street
Ann Arbor, MI 48104

Printed and bound in China

10   9   8   7   6   5   4   3   2   1

Library of Congress Cataloging-in-Publication Data

Schatzer, Jeffery L.
The bump on Santa's noggin: how Santa almost forgot Christmas/ Jeffery L. Schatzer
with Mark Bush and Don Rutt; illustrations by Ty Smith
p. cm.
Summary: When Santa Claus trips over a toy and loses his memory, he gathers clues from others to
learn his own identity, then leaves a special message for the careless boy who caused the trouble.
ISBN-13: 978-1-58726-289-0 (hardcover: alk. paper)
ISBN-10: 1-58726-289-4 (hardcover: alk. paper)
[1. Santa Claus – Fiction. 2. Amnesia – Fiction. 3. Orderliness – Fiction.]
I. Bush, Mark. II. Rutt, Don. III. Smith, Ty, ill. IV. Title
PZ7.S338Bum 2006
[E] – dc22
2006001309

The Bump on Santa's Noggin

How Santa Almost Forgot Christmas

By

Jeffery L. Schatzer

with Mark Bush and Don Rutt

Illustrations by Ty Smith

The Big Belly Series

 mitten press

ilo McMostly was *mostly* good. He ate *most* vegetables without complaining. He went to bed on time *most* every night. Milo was helpful for the *most* part. However, the one job he had the *most* trouble remembering was picking up his stuff.

anta enjoys reading school papers and looking at art projects. One night, Santa was visiting Milo McMostly's school.

Milo's locker was **mostly** messy.

His desk was **mostly** a disaster.

As Santa was looking around the schoolroom, he slipped on a toy that Milo had left on the floor— a **most** unfortunate accident.

ZOOP!

Santa's legs flew out from under him.

WHOOP!

He fell backward.

WHACK!

His head hit the floor.

hen he woke up there was a painful bump on his noggin, and he was very confused. He didn't know who or where he was. All he knew was that he had an important job to do.

After a time he thought to talk to a police officer. They are trained to keep people safe and to help in times of trouble.

"**I** know exactly who you are," said the officer kindly. "Children love to see you each year."

"They do? Why yes, I believe you are correct. I know exactly who I am. Thank you."

"I must be . . .

...a circus performer!

Children love to see the circus."

So he joined the circus as the strongman.

t didn't take long to figure out that he didn't belong in the circus. He wasn't all that strong.

So his quest continued.

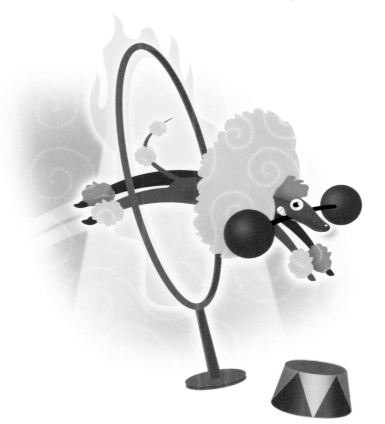

 different thought occured to him. Firefighters do the very important job of putting out fires and rescuing people.

"Maybe a firefighter can help me," he thought.

"Sure," said the firefighter. "I know exactly who you are. You fly through the sky."

"I do? Why yes, I believe you are correct. Thank you."

"I must be . . .

...a superhero!

Superheroes fly through the sky."

e quickly found out that he wasn't a superhero. When he jumped off the porch to fly through the sky, he landed in a pricker bush.

OUCH!

So his quest continued.

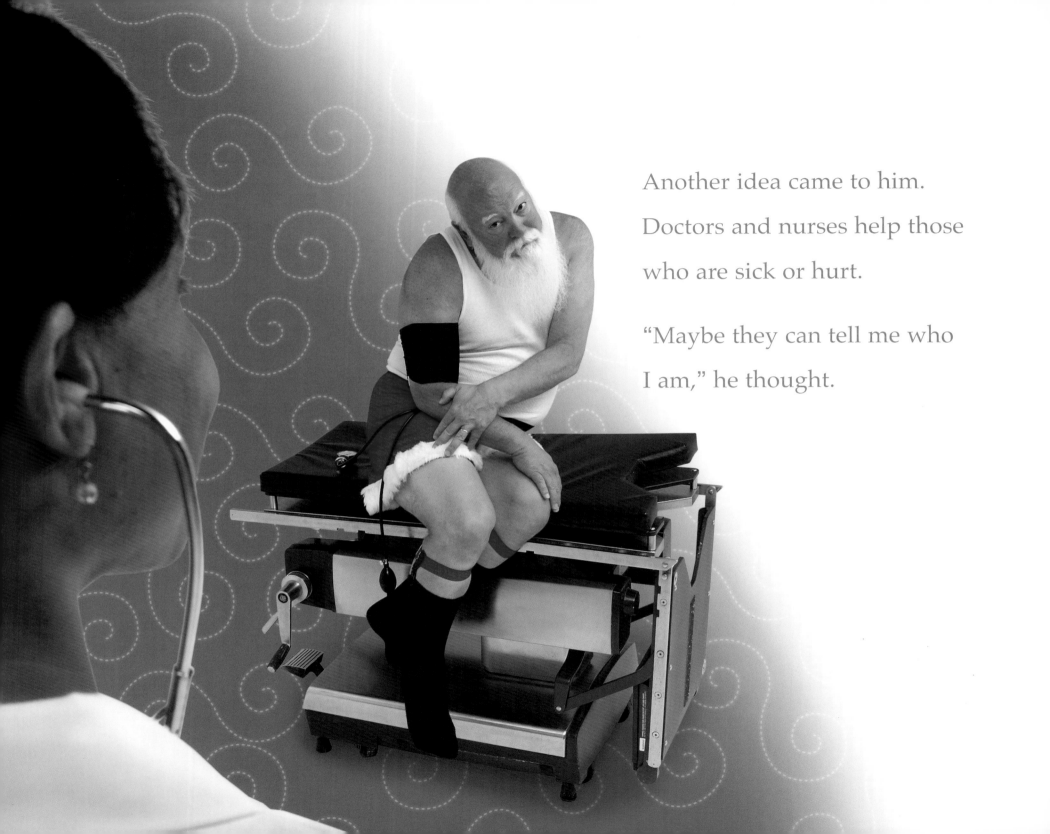

Another idea came to him. Doctors and nurses help those who are sick or hurt.

"Maybe they can tell me who I am," he thought.

know exactly who you are," said the doctor.

"You are the one who leaves surprises for children at night."

"I am? Why yes, I believe you are correct. Thank you."

"I must be . . .

the tooth fairy!

The tooth fairy leaves surprises
for children at night."

t didn't take long to figure out that he wasn't the tooth fairy. For one thing, he didn't like to touch other people's teeth.

Sad and discouraged he walked back to the school where it all started.

"**I**s something wrong?" asked a teacher.

"I can't remember who I am," he answered as he rubbed his noggin. The bump had nearly disappeared, and his head was feeling better.

"What do you know about yourself?"

e counted on his fingers. "I know that children enjoy seeing me each year, but I am not in the circus. I know that I fly through the sky, but I can't fly like a superhero. I know that I deliver surprises to children at night, but I am not the tooth fairy. That's all I know."

Checklist

☑ **Strongman in a Circus**

☑ **Flying Superhero**

☑ **Tooth Fairy**

"There is one more thing," said the teacher wisely. "You have a long, white beard."

BOING!

The answer popped into his head. "I know who I am! I am Santa Claus!" he shouted and jumped for joy.

Santa thanked the teacher. He finally knew who he was and where he had to be. Immediately Santa left for the North Pole and arrived just in time to prepare for Christmas.

That very Christmas Santa left Milo McMostly a note about how important it is to take good care of all of his things–not just *most* of his things.

That's an important lesson for everybody.

Dear Milo,
Please do your best to pick up ALL your things rather than just MOST of your things.

Your friend,

Santa